~NAUGHTY COUPON~

Let Me Deepthroat That Cock

~NAUGHTY COUPON~

Fuck Me Until You Jizz In My Tight Pussy

~NAUGHTY COUPON~

Rail My Pussy Hard And Deep

~NAUGHTY COUPON~

Jizz On My Face

~NAUGHTY COUPON~

Fuck My Tits

~NAUGHTY COUPON~

Let Me Lick Your Balls

~NAUGHTY COUPON~

Fuck My Mouth

~NAUGHTY COUPON~

Lick My Asshole Before You Fuck It

~NAUGHTY COUPON~

I'll Be Loud While You Fuck Me

~NAUGHTY COUPON~

Fuck Me Like A Porn Star

~NAUGHTY COUPON~

Cum In My Asshole

~NAUGHTY COUPON~

Dont Stop Fucking Me Until I Say So

~NAUGHTY COUPON~

Fuck Me Now Daddy

~NAUGHTY COUPON~

Fuck Me Doggystyle

~NAUGHTY COUPON~

Fuck Me Missionary

~NAUGHTY COUPON~

Fuck Me While Standing

~NAUGHTY COUPON~

Record Us Fucking

~NAUGHTY COUPON~

Fuck My Pussy Then Fuck My Asshole

~NAUGHTY COUPON~

Piss In My Mouth

~NAUGHTY COUPON~

I'll Obey All Orders

~NAUGHTY COUPON~

Pull That Dick Out So I Can Give You A Handjob

~NAUGHTY COUPON~

Let Me Ride That Huge Cock

~NAUGHTY COUPON~

Take Pictures Of Me Naked

~NAUGHTY COUPON~

Tie Me Up And Pound This Pussy

~NAUGHTY COUPON~

Jizz Anywhere You Want

~NAUGHTY COUPON~

Lick My Pussy

~NAUGHTY COUPON~

Fuck My Ass Then Mouth

~NAUGHTY COUPON~

Fuck Me In The Shower

~NAUGHTY COUPON~

Jizz On My Tits

~NAUGHTY COUPON~

Pull My Hair And Call Me Dirty Names

~NAUGHTY COUPON~

Let Me Suck Your Dick While You Watch Porn

~NAUGHTY COUPON~

Fuck Me Outside

~NAUGHTY COUPON~

Fuck Me While Watching Porn

~NAUGHTY COUPON~

Fuck Me On The Chair

~NAUGHTY COUPON~

Fuck Me In Front Of The Mirror

~NAUGHTY COUPON~

Fuck Me On The Counter

~NAUGHTY COUPON~

Let's 69

~NAUGHTY COUPON~

Let Me Lick Your Asshole

~NAUGHTY COUPON~

Fuck Me While I Hang Off The Bed

~NAUGHTY COUPON~

Let Me Ride That Dick Reverse Cowgirl

~NAUGHTY COUPON~

Dildo My Pussy While You Fuck My Ass

~NAUGHTY COUPON~

Finger Me While I Suck Your Dick

~NAUGHTY COUPON~

Spank Me

~NAUGHTY COUPON~

Finger My Ass

~NAUGHTY COUPON~

Fuck Me In The Bathtub

~NAUGHTY COUPON~

Blindfold Me Then Fuck Me

~NAUGHTY COUPON~

Pretend I Am Your Celebrity Crush

Printed in Great Britain
by Amazon

37972974R00057